Barbara Kimenye

Paulo's Strange Adventure

Illustrated by
Martin Salisbury

CHELSEA HOUSE PUBLISHERS
New York • Philadelphia

Series Editor: Rod Nesbitt

This edition published 1995 by
Chelsea House Publishers, a division of Main Line Book Co.,
300 Park Avenue South, New York, N.Y. 10010
by arrangement with Heinemann

© Barbara Kimenye 1994

First published by Heinemann International Literature and Textbooks in 1994

ISBN 0-7910-3163-2

Printed and bound in Great Britain by
Cox & Wyman Ltd, Reading, Berkshire

1 3 5 7 9 10 8 6 4 2

CONTENTS

Chapter One	1
Chapter Two	9
Chapter Three	20
Chapter Four	30
Chapter Five	40
Chapter Six	47
Chapter Seven	51
Chapter Eight	59
Chapter Nine	67
Chapter Ten	76
Questions	87
Activities	87
Glossary	89

CHAPTER ONE

Paulo's adventure began because some workmen had left a ladder leaning against a wall. Boys love to climb ladders and this ladder was just waiting to be climbed. If the ladder had not been there or if the boys had not seen it, they would never have tried to climb it, and Paulo would never have slipped and landed himself in a real adventure.

But the ladder was there, leaning up against Mrs Junju's house in the lane along which the boys walked after school, and Richard Ssongo and Basil Basudde, Paulo's friends, quickly spotted it.

'I dare you to climb to the top of that ladder!' Basil cried, turning to Paulo and Richard.

'I bet both of you five shillings each that I can go up and down quicker than either of you!' Richard challenged his friends.

Paulo didn't say a word. He was the smallest of the three boys, and at the age of fourteen he was also the youngest. Paulo had another problem. He was frightened of heights. The mere idea of climbing the tall, steep ladder made him feel a little sick. He felt even worse as he heard Basil eagerly accepting Richard's challenge.

'I'll go first – you time me with your watch,' Basil added.

'But what if Mrs Junju comes out and sees us?' Paulo timidly asked.

'Oh, we're too quick for her,' laughed Richard. 'Anyway, everybody knows that she's as deaf as a stone. She'll never know we are up on her roof.'

Basil went quickly up and down the ladder before anything more could be said.

'Fifty-five seconds,' Richard announced. 'Now let me try. Here. Take the watch and time me.'

He was quicker than Basil. He was up and down the ladder in exactly fifty seconds.

'I knew I would win!' he boasted. 'Come on – hand over your money.'

'Wait a moment. Don't be too quick,' Basil told him. 'You haven't won yet. Paulo still has to show what he can do.'

Paulo swallowed very hard and tried to find a good excuse for not climbing the ladder.

'I'm supposed to be home early today,' he said as fast as he could. 'My mother wants me to help her in the shamba.'

His two friends regarded him and then started to laugh.

'It won't take you an hour to climb the ladder,' Basil said, smiling at Richard. 'You're scared – that's what's wrong with you!'

'No,' Paulo feebly protested, and Richard said, 'Well, if you don't make the climb, you'll still have to hand over five shillings as a forfeit.'

Paulo did not have five shillings, nor was there much chance of his having a lot of money at any time in the near future. From all the things that had happened in the past, he knew how nasty both Richard and Basil could be if he did not obey their wishes. He could picture a beating and some unhappy days ahead for himself if he refused to climb. His fear seemed to give him courage. Clenching his teeth, he held the sides of the ladder with trembling hands. Then he raced up with a speed that came from a feeling of terror rather than any skill in climbing. As he neared the top, he heard Basil yell excitedly, 'Go on, Paulo, keep going – you're beating Richard quite easily!'

The encouragement in Basil's voice was enough to make Paulo forget how scared he was. He glanced down to smile at his friends and that was his mistake. The faces of the two boys, looking up at him, appeared to be hundreds of metres below him. He was drawn towards them, and his head began to spin. He clutched at the ladder, which started to sway in a very frightening way. Then it rocked sideways.

'Look out! Be careful!' warned Basil and Richard. 'Stand still or you'll fall.'

Paulo did not hear what they were saying. He was struggling to keep the ladder upright. He felt dizzy and sick, and he felt his wet, sweaty hands slipping from the ladder. Suddenly, the ladder began to fall backwards, throwing Paulo out over the lane. He sailed through the air and landed with a thud in the back of a heavy lorry which had just driven into the narrow path.

He sailed through the air and landed in the back of a heavy lorry.

Neither Richard nor Basil had noticed the lorry coming up behind them, and they were alarmed to see their friend lying on his back among big sacks of vegetables.

Before the two boys had time to try to understand what had happened, the lorry had gone round a bend in the lane. It quickly disappeared and took Paulo with it. Paulo himself lay stunned and breathless. Then he saw the familiar countryside rushing past him on either side, and he soon realised where he was. His first reaction was to jump down and run home. What stopped him was the steepness of the piled-up sacks of vegetables on which he was lying, and the way in which the lorry went faster and faster as it turned on to the tarmac road. Frightened though he was, there was nothing he could do except hang on till the vehicle made its first stop.

He also kept a worried eye on the dark clouds gathering in the sky and hoped the rain would stay away until he was safely back home. But the weather refused to be kind. Great big raindrops began to fall heavily over everything, and Paulo could only avoid the drenching by forcing his way under some sacks of cabbages.

The nest he made for himself proved warm and more comfortable than he had expected, and very soon he fell fast asleep.

Tired after a long, hard day at school, he slept undisturbed even when the lorry stopped, and the driver and his mate quickly threw a large waterproof cover over their precious load of vegetables. The waterproof cover was supported by a wooden beam which ran from the roof of the lorry's cabin to another fixed upright at the tail-end of the vehicle. It looked exactly like a house, or at least a tent on wheels. This made Paulo's hiding place cosier than ever, and he was so comfortable that he did not even wake up when the lorry stopped again, this time at a small service station for petrol and oil.

It was here that the driver and his mate decided to stroll along to a little café they knew. It was just a short way off the main road and they could walk there in two or three minutes. They left the lorry parked at the service station and asked the service station owner to look after it for them. Then they walked off laughing and talking happily.

Paulo awoke shortly after they had gone, and was very alarmed to find himself in almost complete darkness. He wriggled from under the sacks of vegetables, peered through a hole in the waterproof cover, and saw that it was already twilight.

He knew that his mother would be worrying about him, so he knew that it was important to get home as soon as possible. Then he realised that he had no idea where he was, or which direction to take. He decided to walk back along the road taken by the lorry, and just hope that some kind person would offer him a lift. He crawled towards the back end of the lorry and was about to climb out, when he heard a whispered argument between people standing inches away. This made him stop. He stayed very still. He had never been so frightened in his life.

Two men stood beside the lorry, and every word of their conversation reached Paulo clearly, now that the rain had stopped. It seemed that they were planning to steal the vehicle, and the argument was concerned with whether or not they should wait for another person who had not turned up. They were trying to decide if he would come at all.

'He'll be here any minute. You'll see,' one of the men said confidently. 'I know he won't let us down.'

'But it's nearly seven o'clock,' the other man protested. 'We can't afford to wait any longer. That driver and his mate will be coming back, and– '

'We'll give him another five minutes,' the first man said. 'We need him. Look, I don't want any trouble from Rongo. You know what he's like. I just want to carry out this job without making a mess of everything.'

The other man did not sound very happy. He clearly did not want to wait any longer.

'It's silly to take such a risk,' he said. 'If he can't be here when he promised, why should we wait? I say we either take the lorry, or we go home.'

Paulo heard the argument continuing as the men

moved towards the cabin of the lorry. He wondered frantically what he should do, who he could tell. He thought of shouting to raise the alarm. But supposing there was nobody within earshot? The men he had heard sounded very tough. Then he had another idea. Where had the driver disappeared to? Perhaps he could warn him that these men were about to steal his lorry.

He was still wondering what action to take when he heard shouts and the sound of running feet on the wet road. Then he heard the sound of angry cries. There were grunts and thuds as blows were exchanged, and he heard a man shout out in pain.

Paulo was terrified. He crept back into his hiding place in the vegetable sacks.

He was hiding there when somebody scrambled into the driver's seat. The person started the engine, and the lorry roared away down the road. Paulo hardly noticed the movement. His eyes were fixed in terror on the big man who had thrown himself over the tailboard, and who was now crawling towards him. Paulo was sure he was one of the men who had been planning to steal the lorry.

CHAPTER TWO

Paulo had first seen the man outlined for a moment against the last sunlight glowing in the early evening sky. He was wearing dark trousers and a dark leather jacket. Then, in the gloom caused by the waterproof cover, Paulo could only dimly see a figure crawling towards him.

'Oh no! Please don't hurt me,' Paulo whispered, certain that something terrible was going to happen to him.

At the sound of Paulo's voice, the man stopped as suddenly as if he had received an electric shock.

'Who's there?' he demanded.

Paulo discovered that he was too frightened to speak again. He was shivering and his teeth were chattering so loudly that he was sure the man could hear them. He was sure now that the stranger must be one of the men who had stolen the lorry, and he expected to have his throat cut at any minute. Already the man was near enough to stretch out a hand and touch Paulo's face.

'Why,' the man said in a low voice, 'it's a youngster – a boy, isn't it?'

'Yes – yes, sir,' Paulo managed to stammer.

'What are you doing here?' The man was amazed to find anyone else in the lorry. Doing his best to stop trembling, Paulo told his story as best he could. He kept having to swallow, and occasionally

The man was amazed to find anyone else in the lorry.

lost his voice, because he was still convinced that he was talking to one of the thieves.

'So you've been here since long before my mate and I arrived at the service station. You must have heard us trying to fight when those thugs stole our lorry,' the man said.

Paulo nodded with relief at hearing that he was not, after all, being questioned by one of the crooks.

'I think we're in very serious trouble,' the man murmured to himself. 'I've got to get the lorry back, somehow.' In a louder voice, he added, 'What's your name, son? I'm Matthew, and this lorry belongs to my father.'

Paulo gave Matthew his own name before timidly asking what would happen if the vegetables were not delivered to the market.

'Will your father do something?' he added hopefully. 'Will he go to the police?'

Matthew grunted, and said, 'I suppose the police will soon be on the lookout for us, because those thugs in front...' he pointed at the driver's cabin, '...knocked out my mate, and hit the service station manager with a panga. But we can't be sure that the police will trace us. I think these people are too clever to risk being seen on an open road.'

'You mean we might not get back home?' Paulo choked on the word 'home'.

'We'll do our best. I'll think of something. At least we're lucky that nobody knows that you and I are travelling in the back. It will give us time to make a plan.'

Paulo suddenly found a lump in his throat at Matthew's words.

'Perhaps we should stand near the tailboard, and shout for help at any passing car,' Paulo suggested.

Matthew shook his head firmly. He clearly didn't think this was a good idea.

'Drivers are used to being shouted at and waved at from the backs of lorries,' he said. 'It happens so often that they never take any notice now. They just ignore it.'

'But we must do something!' Paulo cried.

'Don't worry. We will.'

Matthew lit a cigarette, and smoked it in silence. Paulo sat quietly. He was thinking longingly of home and the good supper he was missing. He prayed that Richard and Basil would have enough sense to tell his parents what had happened to him, although he feared that his two friends would be too ashamed to reveal their part in the adventure. They might pretend that they had never seen him. They might even say they knew nothing about where he was.

Meanwhile, the rain started to fall heavily, after the dry spell following the first shower, and the vehicle slid wildly on the muddy surface of the road. Paulo held tightly to the sacks, as he was thrown from side to side. Matthew muttered angrily to himself that the fool at the wheel had not the least idea how to drive a fully loaded lorry. It was a very frightening journey, and it ended quite suddenly and just as frighteningly.

One minute they were rattling along at a terrifyingly fast pace, and the next, the brakes were slammed on so sharply that Paulo and Matthew bounced up into the air. The lorry skidded and slid along the track before the driver managed to stop it.

Matthew thought that a tree must have fallen across the road. However, not long after they stopped, they heard shouts of greeting from people who seemed to be standing all round the vehicle.

'Hide beneath the sacks!' Matthew roughly pushed Paulo down between some bags of spinach and onions, and tried to conceal himself. He was too late. The strong beam of an electric torch suddenly shone full on him, and there was no way for him to escape. He was dragged from the lorry, and the two men who had stolen it were quickly joined by an excited crowd.

'It's the lorry driver!' one of them exclaimed. 'How did he get here?' Then, turning to his partner, he shouted, 'I thought you knocked him out?'

'I did knock him out, Petro. I swear it,' the second man protested. 'You were there. You saw me do it.'

Paulo listened to all this with his heart in his mouth. His fear increased as, from all the shouts and noises around him, he gathered that Matthew was being dragged away, and that he was going to be left completely alone. He waited, trying to hold his breath, for at least five minutes before he dared to creep from his hiding place. Then he carefully made his way to the tailboard of the lorry.

Peering over the edge, he saw that it was parked among a little group of trees. He quickly realised that there was no one in sight, but a smell of wood smoke and cooking floated in the air. In a clearing a short distance away, Paulo also caught a glimpse of a fire, and heard people talking and laughing. His limbs were cramped and stiff as he climbed over the tailboard. He was not at all sure what he should do next, and yet he was sure that he would be safer out of the vehicle, rather than in it. His decision to move proved correct. Hardly had his feet touched the ground than he heard people approaching.

As quickly as he could, he dived underneath the lorry, and crouched in the shelter of one of its huge rear wheels.

He was only just in time. Six men came along, four of whom climbed on to the sacks of vegetables, and began tearing down the tarpaulin.

'It's going to take a bit of time to unload all this stuff, Joe,' one of the other two men said. 'But we'll have to do it, because old Kaddana swears that the cash box is hidden somewhere beneath these sacks.'

'I can't see why everything wasn't taken to the

godown, Rongo. It would be safer and quicker in the long run,' the person addressed as Joe whined.

'Don't be a fool,' Rongo shouted back at him angrily. 'Every policeman in the country will be on the look-out for us. Petro and Musa really ruined things by hanging about waiting for Gitta at the petrol station. Then they had to get involved in a fight. I don't care about them hitting the petrol station owner, but somebody else might have seen them.'

'And what are we going to do with that driver?' Joe wanted to know. 'I don't want anything bad to happen to him.'

'What can we do?' Rongo spoke as though he was tired of the conversation. 'We'll tie him up and leave him with his lorry. By the time he's found, we should be miles away. It's so dark he won't be able to recognise any of us.'

Joe obviously did not like the sound of this arrangement.

'But what if nobody finds him?' he asked in a worried voice.

Rongo gave a nasty laugh. 'Well, that's his bad luck, isn't it?'

Rongo then ordered the men on the lorry to hurl the sacks of vegetables out on to the ground. For what, to Paulo, seemed like hours, they strained, heaved and grunted, pushing and pulling at the heavy sacks. At last one of them gave a loud cry and a shout.

15

'Don't be a fool,' Rongo shouted back at him angrily.

'There's a metal box here. It's wrapped up in a big sack!'

'Pass it down here quickly!' cried Rongo, who appeared to be in charge of everything. 'Come on – get a move on!'

There were further shouts from among the trees and from the fireside, and other men came running.

Paulo, seeing just legs and feet, noticed that only five in a crowd of about twenty wore trousers and shoes. The rest of the thieves were barefoot, and dressed in tattered shorts or grubby kikoyis. Although it was dark enough for him to be well hidden on the inner side of the wheel, he watched the men fearfully as they jumped and yelled excitedly only inches from him.

When at last the crowd moved off, Paulo was tempted to stay where he was. But he had heard what the gang leader intended to do with Matthew. He knew he had to follow Rongo and his friends and do whatever he could to help Matthew escape. Luckily, he was able to keep track of the thieves by slipping quietly after them from tree to tree. And they did not go far. They returned to gather around the fire he had noticed earlier. There was a big spit over the fire. Hanging from it was the carcass of a goat. In pots around the fire they were cooking posho.

The five men wearing trousers sat a little apart from the others, on a fallen log, and Paulo saw that they were examining a large black metal box. From the shelter of the trees, Paulo looked all around for any sign of Matthew, wondering how he would recognise him, for he had never seen him in the light.

Suddenly, Paulo's heart gave a leap. Alongside the log on which the five men sat, lay the still figure of a tall man. In the glow from the fire, Paulo saw that the man's hands and ankles were tied, and the face was bruised and bleeding. It was the leather jacket which provided Paulo with the most important clue. The man lying there was Matthew.

Paulo did not know what to do. He looked from the men and boys gathered round the fire to the group of five sitting on the log. Those by the fire were shouting and laughing. The food was cooked now and they were pushing at each other to try to get near the fire. They pulled pieces of flesh from the carcass of the goat and heaped posho on old plates or banana leaves.

The five men on the log were trying desperately to open the metal box. They were arguing about whether to smash it with a stone or wait for the others to arrive.

The man lying there was Matthew.

CHAPTER THREE

Paulo could not think what to do next. Seeing what had happened to Matthew, he wanted to run away as fast as he could. But he didn't want to be a coward. He couldn't leave Matthew without doing something to try to help him.

'I'll go and find a policeman,' he thought wildly. 'It's all I can do. I'm no use against all those men.'

On the other hand, he realised that he had no idea of where he was. He did not know the direction of the nearest village or town, so he had very little hope of finding a policeman.

He stayed hidden among the trees until a swarm of mosquitoes attacked his face, bare legs and arms. To escape his tormentors he gradually made his way along the edge of the clearing. When he looked up, Paulo found himself only a few feet away from the men sitting on the log. They had their backs to him but Matthew, lying on the ground, was clearly visible in the firelight. Paulo felt much happier when he realised that Matthew's eyelids were moving occasionally. It was as if he was not unconscious, but only pretending to be.

The five men were having a heated argument about who should take care of the cash box. From what they were saying, Paulo understood that they were unable to open it because they could not find the key in any of Matthew's pockets and they had no suitable tools. The one thing they had agreed on was not to smash it with a rock. As they argued, somebody who was obviously in charge of the cooking approached them with chunks of roasted meat and heaps of posho piled on banana leaves. The delicious smell of the food made Paulo's mouth water. He only just stopped himself from rushing forward and grabbing some of the food. All he could do was to sit watching the men greedily chewing the goat and eating the posho. The meat was covered in a spicy sauce which made Paulo even hungrier.

Then in the distance he heard the noise of vehicles arriving on the other side of the clearing. One of the men called out that the Land Rovers were on their way. Immediately the argument going on between the five 'bosses', as Paulo had been calling the men on the log, started up again. It was plain for anyone to see that they did not trust each other, and their main problem seemed to be who should be given the job of hiding the metal box. In the end, they agreed to draw lots to decide who it would be. But whoever was chosen to do the job would be guarded by two of the other 'bosses' until it was safe to recover the box and somehow open it.

In spite of his fear, Paulo was fascinated by the idea of drawing lots. This was something he had never seen or heard of before. He held his breath as the cook brought a handful of dried grass, and each of the five men took one of the stems. The winner was the man they called Joe, a big fat man. When he shouted that he had drawn the longest stem of grass, Paulo realised that made him the winner. The other men were not happy, but they had agreed to draw lots and there was nothing they could do now. They sat and watched as Joe went over to the metal box. The box was heavy, and an awkward size. Joe tried to pick it up in his arms, but it was too big to hold. He tried to drag it, but it caught in the grass and the roots of the trees. At last he found that the easiest way to carry it was on his head. Two of the other men helped him to lift it up and then balance it carefully.

At any other time, Paulo might have laughed at the sight of this fat man walking between the trees with a box on his head, and using an electric torch to find his way forward. Paulo followed him along a narrow path, across a swamp where large flat stones laid between tall reeds and bulrushes were the only means of crossing, and finally into the depths of a thick forest.

In the forest, Paulo had a few moments of panic, for quite suddenly Joe disappeared. Then he saw him again. He was examining a gigantic tree. But no sooner had Paulo caught sight of him, than he moved around behind the tree, and neither he nor his torch could be seen.

Paulo stared as hard as he could into the darkness, but it was as if Joe had just disappeared.

Paulo didn't know what to do. If he was going to help Matthew, he needed to find that box.

'Surely he hasn't climbed the tree?' he asked himself. 'He couldn't, not with that heavy box.' He was just about to creep forward to investigate when the beam of the torch appeared in the darkness again, and Joe came out from behind the tree. He was no longer carrying the metal box.

Paulo was not sure of the way back, so he did not want to lose sight of Joe. Nevertheless, he waited till Joe was some way ahead, then ran to the tree and tore two broad strips off the bark. This would help to tell him where Joe had hidden the box. As soon as he had marked the tree, he silently followed Joe back to where the other men waited.

It was a good thing that Paulo acted quickly, because Joe had been very cunning. He took a different path on the way back. Paulo realised that he was trying to make the other men believe that he was returning from a different direction from where he had really been.

Once more, Paulo edged his way to his place behind the men sitting on the log. No sooner had he reached there than a short man in a shabby tweed jacket worn over a grimy kanzu came and stood near the group. He could not stand still and moved nervously from one foot to the other. This man was obviously anxious to have a word with Rongo, and it seemed to Paulo that Matthew, still helpless on the ground, was the reason for his not wishing to come too close. The man immediately relaxed when a couple of the thieves were called to take Matthew away and throw him in the back of his lorry.

As the thugs were carrying Matthew off, the man dashed forward.

'I've come for my money, Rongo, sir,' he said in a nervous voice. He bent forward, rubbing his hands together. He almost fell on his knees. 'You know I am poor– '

Rongo rudely interrupted him with a wave of his hand.

'You'll get your money all right, Kaddana. I've already told you it will be delivered to you by sundown tomorrow.'

'But you promised I could have it as soon as the job was finished,' Kaddana reminded him.

'I said as soon as everything was settled,' Rongo told him. 'Now, go home and mind your own business. Don't worry. You'll be paid.'

Paulo saw that Kaddana was frightened, yet the man stubbornly stayed where he was.

'Why can't I be paid now?' he demanded.

Rongo angrily jumped to his feet, and for the first time Paulo had a good view of him. He thought the man looked very tough and very frightening.

'Go home. If you stay here annoying us much longer, you'll regret it,' Rongo snarled. Kaddana walked slowly away, his hands in his pockets and his eyes looking around nervously.

Although Paulo had watched the discussion between Rongo and Kaddana with interest, he was more concerned with how and when to rescue Matthew. He was still without a definite plan when Rongo signalled for the fire to be stamped out, and everybody prepared to leave. The crowd of ragged men wandered off, either alone or in twos and threes, after receiving money from Rongo. At least, Paulo thought they were being given money, because he saw Rongo hand each of them something. Kaddana did not get anything. Obviously he would get his share when the box was opened.

The bosses then walked off together to where Matthew's lorry was parked. As he followed them, Paulo noticed two Land Rovers drawn up beside it. He watched the five men climb into the vehicles and drive away. Paulo noticed that two of the men got into one of the Land Rovers with Joe. They still did not trust him, and they were not going to let him out of their sight. Before they left, they removed the battery from the lorry's engine compartment.

Paulo could have cried as he watched this happen, for it meant that the vehicle was useless, and there was no hope of Matthew driving it home. He hid for another few minutes, to make sure that the gang really had gone, and then he climbed on to the vehicle and almost fell over Matthew lying bound and gagged.

Paulo dragged away the piece of dirty cloth covering Matthew's mouth.

Quickly, Paulo dragged away the piece of dirty cloth covering Matthew's mouth, and started undoing the ropes tying his wrists. The moment his hands were free, Matthew quickly started untying his own ankles.

He and Paulo wasted no time in talking, until they were out of the lorry and safely hidden among the trees. Then Paulo told Matthew about the battery being removed from the lorry. Matthew had suspected that this would happen but he said nothing about it. Instead he put his hand on Paulo's shoulder.

'I'll never forget you, son,' he said, as he searched for cigarettes and matches. 'You saved my life, and no mistake. I was a fool to allow myself to be caught in the first place.'

'Are you sure you're all right?' Paulo anxiously asked him. 'There's blood over your right eye, and your mouth is terribly swollen.'

Paulo lit a match and looked at Matthew's wounds closely. Then, taking a clean handkerchief Matthew had given him, he wet it in some rain water trapped in one of the big leaves on the ground. He washed the blood away as carefully as he could and looked at the wounds again.

'Your eye is cut,' he said, 'and there's a big bruise on your forehead. Your mouth isn't cut, but it looks very sore.'

Matthew shrugged his shoulders and smoked his cigarette.

'I'm not feeling exactly on top of the world,' he admitted. 'But I don't think there is anything seriously wrong with me. I'm more worried about the cash box those crooks stole than I am about my personal beauty. What I don't understand is how they could have known the cash box was on the lorry in the first place.'

'The cash box!' Paulo almost shouted in his excitement. 'I know where it is! I followed the man called Joe, and saw where he hid it. At least, I– '

'You did what?' It was Matthew's turn to be excited. The cigarette dropped from his fingers as he grasped Paulo firmly by the shoulders. 'Where is it?' He gave the boy a slight shake. 'Are you sure you know?'

Paulo hesitated and did not speak for a moment.

'Well, I can't honestly say I could lead you straight to the spot. It was as dark as it is now. I think, though, that I could find a tree near to where Joe put the box – I marked it by tearing off some pieces of bark. We should be able to find that.'

He then described how he trailed Joe and watched Joe's surprising vanishing trick.

Matthew nodded in a pleased way, and said, 'You did well. No, you did better than that. I want you to know that you have proved a blessing to me as well as all the good people who have money in that cash box. Come on. Lead the way. The sooner we collect it, the better. I'm certain that some of the thieves will try to get the money for themselves.

There'll be more money for them if they don't have to share it.'

Because they had no light, they had to move much more slowly than when Paulo had followed Joe and his torch. But they soon found the stepping stones across the swamp. They stopped for a few minutes by a stream at the edge of the forest, and Matthew lay down and bathed his battered face in the cold water again. Once in the forest, they walked slowly, groping their way between the trees, and running their fingers over the bark for signs of recent scars. It was very slow work. They could not rush in case they missed the place where Paulo had torn the bark away.

Suddenly, Paulo called softly to Matthew that he believed he had found the tree for which they were searching.

Matthew stumbled to his side, and was ready to strike a match. Then he stiffened, and seconds later pulled Paulo quickly behind the wide trunk of a tree which grew alongside the one Paulo thought he had identified.

'What's wrong?' Paulo whispered.

Matthew placed his mouth close to Paulo's ear, and replied, 'I think we've been followed.'

Even as he spoke, they heard footsteps approaching through the thick grass and scrub. Then they saw the beam of an electric torch through the trees.

CHAPTER FOUR

Paulo was frightened. His legs were shaking, and he could feel cold sweat trickling down between his shoulder blades as the footsteps drew nearer.

Neither he nor Matthew had the courage to try to see who it was coming close to them. From the murmur of voices as the men approached, they guessed that there were at least two of them, possibly three.

'Where else could he have hidden the box?' they heard somebody remark. 'I'm sure this is the place, and I don't think he could have buried it because he wasn't carrying a spade.'

Somebody else said, 'He could have put it in the stream, or hidden it along that steep part of the bank. That's the sort of thing he would do.'

What helped Matthew and Paulo to breathe more easily was the knowledge that they were not the reason for the hunt. Instead, they were witnessing the truth of the old saying, 'There's no honour among thieves'. The men they could hear were clearly members of the gang. Both Matthew and Paulo knew that they were looking for the cash box so that they would not have to share the money with Joe and the others.

All the same, with these people searching, and flashing the torch everywhere, Paulo and Matthew had several frightening moments. At one point, the men actually came to examine the roots of the tree behind which the two of them were hiding, and Paulo and Matthew had to quietly move around it to avoid being found. They lay close to the ground, as still as possible, trying not even to breathe.

They only relaxed after the men gave up the search, and went to look for the box elsewhere.

'What did I tell you?' Matthew said, as soon as he and Paulo were alone. 'I knew that some of them would not be able to resist trying to find the box before the time came to share the money.'

'I ... I thought they were after us,' Paulo stammered.

'So did I,' Matthew replied in a low voice. 'Anyway, now they have gone, let's have another look at the tree which you thought you recognised.'

The marks on the bark of the tree which Paulo had found before he and Matthew were disturbed proved to be the ones he had made earlier. By the dim light of a match, they could clearly see the two fresh scars in the trunk of the tree.

'You're a brilliant boy!' Matthew exclaimed. 'Now, you said that Joe suddenly disappeared, and we have to know where he vanished to – it couldn't have been far.'

They walked round and round the tree, but they could not see where Joe could have hidden the box. It looked just like an ordinary tree. But then Matthew pushed aside a thick growth of wild orchids hanging down over the trunk. He felt around for a moment and then turned and whispered excitedly to Paulo. He pointed down at the trunk of the tree.

'Look at this – this tree is hollow! The insides are all rotted away.'

He quickly lit another match, and they both peered into the great hollow trunk. There, standing on one end, was the cash box. Paulo wriggled into the hole and began to push at the box. Matthew tugged at it and together they were able to push and pull it free.

'We've got it, son. Thanks to you!' Matthew panted, patting Paulo's shoulder.

Although Paulo was proud of his part in the recovery of the cash box, his first question was, 'Can we go home now?'

'Of course we can go home,' Matthew told him, laughing and panting at the same time. 'Just as soon as we've reported this nasty business to the police.'

Paulo's mouth drooped and he gave a deep sigh.

'Oh, can't we do that tomorrow? You'll never believe how hungry I am. I was late for lunch at school, and there were only scraps left by the time I got to the dining hall.'

Matthew laughed. 'I'd forgotten that schoolboys are always hungry, and I did have a snack with my mate in the café before we ran into those thieves.'

He thought for a moment or two, then said, 'I wonder if my mate left any food in the cabin of the lorry? He usually carries a bit of something with

'We've got it, son. Thanks to you!' Matthew panted.

him, because he never stops eating. Come on, we'll go and try to find something to fill that hole in your tummy.'

It was hard work carrying the box through the forest back to the lorry. Both Paulo and Matthew were out of breath by the time they arrived, and thankfully dropped the box to the ground. At the spot where the gang had feasted, they found a banana leaf holding two large, untouched slices of goat meat. Some ants had already started on the meat, but Paulo was too hungry to care about them. He brushed them off the meat, and ate it with great enjoyment.

'You really are hungry,' Matthew observed, shaking his head. 'I hope we can find some food in the lorry, before you start eating me!'

Laughing, they walked to the vehicle, and Paulo grinned with delight when Matthew climbed into the driver's cabin and handed him two buns, a bag of groundnuts and a great juicy mango.

They sat on the ground, their backs against one of the wheels, and shared this food.

'Now, tell me again how you came to be lying among the vegetable sacks,' Matthew said to Paulo. 'It was very, very lucky for me that you got into the lorry. If you hadn't been there, I would still be lying helpless, expecting to die of starvation. All I could do would be to pray somebody might come along and find me before it was too late. The cash box would have been lost for ever.'

Paulo told Matthew his story again. Although the fall from the ladder had frightened him, that was not the worst part. What had really worried him was seeing Matthew lying at the feet of the thugs, looking as if he was dead.

'They're horrible people,' he said. 'Why, even that little man who came to ask for his money looked as though he was terrified of them. That man, Rongo, only spoke a few words to him, and he frightened him to death.'

Matthew frowned. 'I didn't see that man, and yet I'll swear I recognised his voice. Did you manage to get a good look at him?'

Paulo nodded. 'I saw him clearly. He was small, and wore a tweed jacket with a big hole in the elbow of one sleeve. His kanzu was the dirtiest I have ever seen in my life.'

'Was his hair long and thick?' Matthew asked.

'I don't really know,' Paulo answered truthfully. 'The fire lit up his clothes and his face. I didn't pay any attention to his hair. But I do remember that he had a very thin, long nose.' He paused, making a big effort to remember something else about the little man. Then, 'Wait a minute! I remember now! Rongo called him Kaddana!'

Matthew jumped to his feet.

'Yes, you're right, it was Kaddana!' he cried. 'I knew I recognised that voice. I was dazed, and yet that voice reminded me of somebody. Kaddana of all people. Who would have thought it?' He turned to Paulo. 'He's very well liked by the other farmers, and only last month he was elected to the management committee of our co-operative society.'

'Are you sure it's the same man?' Paulo sounded doubtful. 'The one I was telling you about didn't look very respectable. He was so dirty. And I could have misheard the name.'

'I'm sure of it,' Matthew insisted. 'Kaddana is always dirty. People say he only washes once a month. But he's a very good farmer.' He thought for a while. 'And, of course, he must have been the one who told the crooks that I was carrying the money under the vegetable sacks. How else would they know?'

'Yes, it must be the same man,' Paulo agreed, 'and he did tell them about the money. I heard Rongo say so when they were throwing the sacks down.'

He repeated to Matthew as much as he could remember of the conversation he had overheard while he was hiding underneath the lorry. Then he said that he was curious to know how a boxful of money came to be travelling in the company of sacks of vegetables.

'I'll tell you as we're looking for the nearest police post,' Matthew promised, pulling Paulo to his feet. 'We'd better get started. No time to lose!'

They set off, following the tyre tracks made by the lorry. It was no easier carrying the box now than it had been in the forest.

Puffing and panting, Matthew explained that the box contained money which the Njogo Farmers' Co-operative Society intended to use to buy a tractor. Matthew and his father had regularly advised the members to keep their money in the national bank, but most of them were too old-fashioned to trust the banks. They had insisted that Matthew carry the cash they had saved to Kampala for the purchase of the new tractor. Kaddana, Matthew was certain, had lost no time in informing the gang how the money was being transported.

As Matthew talked, thick black clouds moved across the starlit sky and flew quickly across the face of the recently risen moon. Soon it was impossible to see more than one or two metres ahead.

Matthew and Paulo had been hoping that the tyre tracks would lead them to the main road. Their progress had been slow but steady, but the inky darkness caught them at a place where the track branched in three separate directions. To add to their problems, great drops of rain bounced down, lightning streaked above, and a deafening clap of thunder made them run for the shelter of a bush.

'We shouldn't be near trees during a thunderstorm,' Paulo said. His teeth were chattering so hard with the cold that he could hardly speak.

Matthew tried to make a joke to stop Paulo from worrying. He said that he would rather be struck by lightning than be drowned in a river of rain water.

'I don't want to die at all,' Paulo replied. 'But I'm quite a good swimmer, so I don't think I'll drown.'

Matthew looked around and peered into the darkness.

'If the rain doesn't stop soon,' he said, 'this track will really turn into a river. Then you can show me how well you can swim.'

The downpour increased, and the bush under which they were sheltering gave them very little protection. They talked for a few more minutes and then decided to continue walking. They might, Matthew hopefully suggested, come across a house and be offered shelter. Ankle deep in mud, they plodded along in silent, wet misery. Then far ahead of them something sparkled in the rain. They soon saw the welcome sight of lamplit windows in the distance. This gave them new energy, and they quickened their pace.

Not far from the homestead, Matthew suddenly decided that it might be better to hide the cash box before asking for shelter against the storm.

'Why?' Paulo asked in amazement. 'I think it would be much safer with us – if the people living there let us in.'

'We can't afford to take any more risks,' Matthew told him. 'I just don't trust anybody any more. I know it's only my imagination, but I feel everyone is trying to steal this money.'

So the cash box was left in the swirling brown

waters of a ditch overhung with drooping ferns. When they were satisfied that it could not easily be seen, Matthew and Paulo walked up the broken gravel driveway to the house. At their approach, a dog barked menacingly, and a nightwatchman with a blanket over his head came towards them, a lantern in his hand.

'Who are you, and what do you want here?' The man spoke in a rough voice, and he was clearly not happy to see them. He stood in front of them and held the lantern up to see their faces.

Just as Matthew started to answer him, the door of the house opened, and the figure of another man appeared in the doorway.

'Who's there, Elijah?' the man called out. 'Is it somebody with a message for me?'

The nightwatchman shouted something in reply, but Paulo was not listening to him. Instead, he was staring at the figure in the doorway. Then he took hold of Matthew's arm and pulled him around. He was so excited he could hardly speak.

'That man at the door is Joe – the one who hid the box in the tree. I'm certain of it!'

CHAPTER FIVE

There was no time for Matthew and Paulo to think about the shock of coming face to face with Joe. Joe was still standing in the doorway looking out at them. He was repeating the nightwatchman's questions about who they were, and what they wanted.

Matthew pulled Paulo out of the light coming from the house, and shouted, 'It's all right. We're sorry to bother you. We were looking for Mr Kaligizo. Does he live anywhere around here?'

Joe shook his head.

'No, he doesn't. There are only two other houses in this area, and nobody of that name lives in either of them.'

'I'm sorry if we've caused you any trouble.' Matthew pulled Paulo away from the house. He continued to talk over his shoulder as they walked back down the pathway. 'We must have misunderstood Kaligizo when he gave us the directions to his house.'

'Just a minute,' Joe shouted after them. He started to come out into the rain. 'I think we've met before. From what I can see of you, you look familiar. Where have we met before?'

'I have a twin brother,' laughed Matthew. He quickened his stride and pulled Paulo after him. They broke into a trot, hurrying down the path.

They ignored Joe's shouts for them to stop.

They splashed their way down the muddy driveway, and kept going until they felt they were safely away from Joe and his house. When they stopped, they were just opposite the place where they had hidden the metal box. They stood panting, both of them bent over with their hands on their knees.

'That was Joe, all right,' Paulo gasped when he could speak again. 'And it won't be long before he remembers where he has seen you, Matthew.'

Matthew impatiently wiped the driving rain from his face, and said, 'I know. And it won't be long before he comes after us. The good thing is that we know where at least one member of the gang lives, and the information will be useful if we can find a police post.'

A gleam of car headlamps appeared along the road behind them, and they heard the roar of the engine as it headed their way. Without another word, they dived into the ditch where they had hidden the cash box, and lay in the muddy water until the car passed by. The driver was going slowly and Paulo could see Joe and the watchman in the car. They were peering out into the night, trying desperately to see any movement in the darkness.

By the time Matthew and Paulo had dragged the cash box back on to the road, they were even wetter than ever, and they were both shivering with

They lay in the muddy water until the car passed by.

cold. Matthew's leather jacket was completely soaked now and the water ran down from Paulo's shirt and trousers.

They struggled on down the road, carrying the box with them. Paulo was sure that it was becoming heavier with every step. But they kept going. Their only wish was to get as far away from Joe as they could.

'If we stay on the road, they'll soon find us,' Matthew said. 'I think we should go across country and try to find a main road.'

Paulo was so tired that he just wanted to lie down. If only they could find somewhere dry!

'Let's find somewhere to rest,' he said. 'We can go faster when the rain stops.'

'It will also be easier for them to find us in daylight,' replied Matthew. 'I think we should try to find the police as quickly as possible.'

Paulo was too tired to argue any more. They picked up the box and turned off the road. Pushing with all their strength, they forced their way through a thick hedge of elephant grass, and came to a stretch of uncultivated land. The rain slackened, and the black clouds gave way to bright moonlight, revealing a sharp rise in the land in front of them.

'If we can climb that hill, we will probably come to a main road,' Matthew said. 'Shall we try it?'

'Yes, let's,' Paulo said. 'The further away we can get from Joe's house the better I'll feel.' Nervously, he added, 'You don't think he will see us on the road, do you? He was driving the car that came after us, you know...'

Matthew tried to give Paulo courage. He was not very happy himself, but he did not want Paulo to be terrified.

'Are you sure that it was Joe in the car? It could have been someone else. I know you said it was Joe, but it was very dark. We'll take a chance. I know plenty of lorry drivers, and if we wave one down, he'll give us a lift.'

They walked on in silence. Paulo was still worried, and his arm was aching from the weight of the box. He did his best to keep up with Matthew's long stride, but suddenly he tripped over a large stone, and fell headlong.

When Matthew helped him to his feet, Paulo gave a sharp cry of pain as his left foot touched the ground.

'What's wrong?' Matthew anxiously asked him, and Paulo groaned, 'My ankle – it hurts.'

'Let me see it.'

Paulo balanced himself against the box, and obediently held out his ankle for Matthew's inspection.

'Mmmm,' Matthew said at last. 'You seem to have sprained it. We'll have to hide the box here, because you won't be able to help carry it. Hold on to me. I'll take your full weight so you'll be able to walk.'

'No, Matthew.' Paulo gritted his teeth against the pain. 'You'll be able to move faster without me. We have to think of the farmers whose savings are in the box. Go and find a police post. I'll stay here on guard.'

'A fine guard you would be, with a sprained ankle. I don't think you could do much against Rongo and his friends!' Matthew commented. 'We are in this together, son. So if I go, you're coming with me.'

No argument of Paulo's could change Matthew's mind. Then Matthew had an idea. He suggested that a tight bandage might ease the pain in Paulo's ankle, and that a stick would help him to walk.

'If you can get along comfortably like that, I'll carry the cash box on my head. Joe isn't the only person who can do it, you know!' he added. Paulo thought it was a great idea. So Matthew made a bandage out of a couple of oily rags he took from one of his pockets.

'My ankle feels better already,' Paulo told him.

'Right,' Matthew replied. 'Now wait here. I'll go and break a branch off one of those trees over there. It won't be a smart walking stick, but it will do the job all the same.'

Leaving Paulo sitting on the cash box, Matthew ran to a group of trees and walked around them, looking for a branch suitable for a walking stick. Matthew was looking closely at the trees and did not see what was happening behind him. Paulo could only stare as the heads and shoulders of four men rose like shadows over the brow of the little hill behind Matthew. At first, Paulo thought they were the shadows of the trees in the moonlight. But then they hurried from boulder to boulder down the hill and leapt upon Matthew, pulling him down and jumping on him. Paulo's warning shout died in his throat. He was speechless with terror.

Matthew put up a good fight, but he did not stand a chance against four big men, two of whom were armed with pangas. Within minutes, he was dragged struggling up and over the hill, and Paulo was left staring at the empty countryside.

There was no doubt in his mind that Joe had alerted the rest of the gang, and the four men were part of the search party out looking for him and Matthew. He wondered how long it would be before they came back for him.

CHAPTER SIX

Then Paulo remembered the cash box, and it seemed terribly important that the gang did not get their greedy hands on it again.

He looked around. In the darkness, even with the moon shining now, there was not much to see. Ahead of him was the top of the hill Matthew and he had been climbing. On his left the land seemed to stretch far into the distance. There was nowhere to hide in that direction. On his right were the trees Matthew had been looking at when he was attacked.

Paulo limped over to the trees and peered into the shadows. He realised that he was looking into a forest. Matthew had only examined the few trees growing at one end. Slowly, Paulo walked a little way into the forest. It was even darker now, but he could see that there were lots of places to hide. There were trees with low branches, and thick bushes grew in between the trees. There were heaps of wet leaves and broken branches. If he could get the box into the trees, he could hide it in any of a hundred places.

He limped back to the box and sat down on it. Slowly, he moved his sprained ankle. In spite of the bandage, the pain hit him sharply whenever he moved his foot. He got up and took one of the handles at the side of the box. He started to pull.

He decided to try pushing it.

As soon as he put his weight on his sore ankle a terrible pain shot up his leg. He stopped and sat gasping on the ground. It was clear that he would not be able to drag the box to safety.

So, after a few experiments, he decided to try pushing it. Although this meant having to crawl on the muddy track, and his ankle was not free from pain, the cash box slid forward more easily than Paulo had expected. His hardest task was to keep it from sliding sideways away from the forest and down the hill.

About an hour after starting on this crawl-and-push journey, his arms and legs were so tired that he was glad to rest for a few minutes. At first he had looked around every few seconds to watch for the men who had attacked Matthew. Surely they would be coming back for the box. But when he saw no sign of them, he soon forgot about them as he pushed at the heavy metal box.

Now he looked around again. Why had they not come back? They had probably not seen him in the darkness. He had been sitting quietly on the ground watching Matthew. But why did they not come back to search for the box? Then Paulo knew why. They were waiting for daylight. They knew the box would not be far away. It would be much easier to find it in the daylight.

Paulo looked at the sky. The moon had gone now, and away to the east the sky looked lighter. He had only two or three hours to hide the box.

He began to push at the box again. His knees were sore and bruised, and his hands and arms soon ached again. Finally he pushed the box past the first trees and into the forest. It was harder now. He had to push the box round trees and bushes. Then to his delight he found that the box slid quite easily on the thick layer of wet leaves. He pushed until he was completely exhausted, and then he lay panting on a bed of soft, damp moss in the middle of a clump of bushes.

He only intended to rest long enough to ease his throbbing ankle and his aching back and arms. He closed his eyes while he thought very carefully of what action he should take to try to find help for Matthew.

He fell asleep without knowing it, and awoke at dawn, chilled to the bone.

In the branches of the tallest bush sat several birds. They seemed to be watching him. After a few moments they began to play a game. Paulo smiled at them as they jumped from branch to branch, chirping and whistling. They seemed to be calling and talking to each other. Then a movement and a rustle of leaves nearby caught his attention. He turned quickly, and there, staring at him through the foliage, and holding a well-sharpened knife, was the strangest man Paulo had ever seen.

CHAPTER SEVEN

In the early morning light, the stranger's thick hair looked like coarse fur, hanging raggedly around his face. A length of bark cloth, tied at one shoulder and fastened at the waist by a piece of rope, fell almost to his ankles. His face and what could be seen of his body were covered with pale clay.

He and Paulo looked at each other for a long time in silence, but when the man made as if to come near him, Paulo fell back with a cry of fear.

'No! No! Keep away from me!'

The man stood still for a moment. Then he spoke in a surprisingly gentle voice.

'You needn't be afraid. I won't hurt you. I am Muntole, Guardian of this Sacred Grove. Every tree, plant and creature living here is in my care. Now that you have come, I must protect you, too.'

Paulo was not sure if he believed this. He thought he was either dreaming, or facing a madman. He sat close to the cash box, as the man slowly walked towards him. He was terrified again. He seemed to have spent the last twelve hours being terrified. He only relaxed a little when the man placed the knife into a sheath attached to the rope around his waist. He pulled himself back against the box, however, as the man sat down beside him. But it was only for a moment.

Paulo fell back with a cry of fear.

Muntole's presence gave Paulo a feeling of peace such as he sometimes felt in the company of his mother. It made him feel that he was safe and that no harm would come to him. He looked at Muntole curiously, no longer afraid of him.

The peaceful silence of the forest was disturbed when a flock of small, brightly coloured birds settled near Muntole, and chirped loudly at him. He produced a handful of seeds from a pouch, also attached to the rope around his waist, and scattered them on the ground. The birds eagerly pecked the seeds and, after finishing them, fluttered all over Muntole, occasionally perching on his head, shoulders and wrists.

'That is as much as you will get from me today,' he told them, pretending to be angry with them. 'You will forget how to find food for yourselves, if you have to depend upon me all the time.'

'They don't seem at all nervous or afraid,' Paulo remarked, staring in amazement at two little birds who poked their beaks enquiringly into the pocket of his shirt.

Muntole smiled. 'Why should they be afraid? As I told you, nothing can hurt them here. This is the Sacred Grove. It is a holy place, a place of peace. And I am Muntole, Guardian of the Sacred Grove.'

For some reason he could not explain, Paulo was embarrassed by Muntole's words. To Paulo's mind, it did not fit with what he knew of the modern world, in which radio, television, air travel, and even journeys into outer space were accepted as normal events. Muntole talked as if there was some magic in the trees. He seemed to think this place was perfectly safe from any danger. Paulo suspected Muntole was a little strange in the head – rather like one of his own uncles who believed himself to be the Pope.

However, Paulo kept his thoughts to himself. He didn't want to make Muntole angry, not with that knife in his belt. Then Muntole said something which made Paulo much more cheerful.

'I have fed my small friends,' he said, 'and now I must look after you. Come, let us breakfast together.'

He rose easily to his feet, but as Paulo tried to stand, the same terrible pain shot through his sprained ankle. He stumbled, and came down heavily on the cash box. Immediately, he was reminded of Matthew. He sat staring at the ground. How could he have forgotten his new friend? He was ashamed to have been lying around in this so-called sacred grove, looking forward to breakfast, while his friend, Matthew, was at the mercy of a gang of crooks.

'I see you have hurt your ankle – or is it your foot?' Muntole bent to remove the oily rags around Paulo's ankle.

Paulo miserably shook his head, and blinked the tears from his eyes.

'My ankle doesn't matter,' he said with a sob. 'I

must get help for my friend ... He is ...'

'Wait.' Muntole held up his hand for silence. 'First allow me to attend to your ankle. Then I will give you food, and we will talk.'

'But this is urgent!' Paulo started to protest.

Muntole placed a hand on Paulo's head, and said quietly, 'Trust me.'

Strangely enough, Paulo found that he did trust this strange little man. He sat quietly as Muntole examined his ankle, and waited patiently when, without a word, Muntole left him alone for a few minutes, returning with several long purple leaves and a handful of wet brown clay. He skilfully applied the wet clay and leaves to Paulo's foot, ankle, and the lower part of his leg. The soothing coolness of this mixture quickly eased the pain, and Muntole promised him that he would be able to walk without too much discomfort as soon as the clay dried.

'Is it a special kind of clay?' Paulo wanted to know.

'A very special kind, and found only near the oldest tree in this grove,' Muntole replied, and pointed to the smears on his own body. 'This is the same clay. As you see, it loses its colour as it dries. I wear it whenever I am searching for honey. It makes the bees friendly.

'Now, rest your ankle. I will bring breakfast here, because my house is too far away for you to walk there at the moment.'

He went off between the bushes and trees, leaving Paulo to watch the interesting behaviour of some of the creatures who lived in the sacred grove. He was astonished at the way they behaved. It was as if they had been friends for a long time. A fat rabbit hopped casually over his outstretched legs, a curious mongoose sniffed at the cash box, and ground squirrels chased each other around him. Time passed quickly, and Paulo was taken by surprise when Muntole appeared, carrying honeycombs, a gourd of goat's milk, and several flat, greyish loaves of bread wrapped in banana leaves.

'I am very proud of my bread,' he declared, as he spread the feast on the ground, and smiled. 'I make it from wild corn. I hope you like it.'

Paulo thought it was the best bread he had ever tasted, and he said so. Then he remembered the meal he had shared with Matthew, the two of them leaning with their backs against the lorry, and the memory completely spoiled his appetite.

Putting aside the tasty bread, he told Muntole his story, up to the point where Matthew had been attacked and taken away by the gang, and Paulo himself had crawled with the cash box to the sacred grove.

'You're perfectly safe here,' Muntole assured him, as Paulo reached the end of the tale.

'I know I am safe, the money is safe ... but what about Matthew, my friend?' Paulo cried.

Muntole briefly closed his eyes, and said, 'I'm thinking of Matthew. My brother is a policeman. He will know what to do.'

Paulo tried to struggle to his feet. 'Where is he? I must see him at once. There's no time to lose!'

Muntole got up quickly and eased him back to a sitting position.

'My brother is in Kampala,' he said quietly.

'Kampala!' echoed Paulo. 'That's miles away! He'll never get here in time to save Matthew.'

'Be patient,' Muntole advised him. 'I have an idea. My brother will be with us by noon.'

Paulo was bewildered. He said, 'How can he? I mean, I don't understand how you can reach him. Do you have a telephone?'

Muntole shook his head. 'I don't have a telephone. I have something more reliable.'

He stood up, and whistled a long clear note. Nothing happened for about a minute, then a flutter of wings told them of the approach of a beautiful pearl-coloured pigeon which settled on Muntole's shoulder. She sat there, quite happily, preening herself, cooing softly, and now and again rubbing her back on Muntole's ear.

Paulo was mystified. 'I still don't understand,' he said.

'Don't you?' Muntole ran a finger over the bird's downy neck. 'This is Sara. She is my brother's special friend and always knows where to find him. She often carries messages between us. We will send her to him now.'

It was too much for Paulo. What was he doing, wasting precious time with a madman who expected a pigeon to find somebody in the heart of a city? Suddenly Paulo could stand it no longer. He jumped to his feet, ignoring the pain in his ankle. He waved his arms about wildly, the tears running down his face.

'You don't understand!' he shouted at Muntole. 'You don't know what's happening. Matthew needs help and you're going to send a pigeon to find your brother in Kampala? You're crazy! You're completely crazy!'

CHAPTER EIGHT

Muntole allowed Paulo to cry until his wild sobs died away and became weary hiccups. He watched the boy for some time, with a strange look in his eyes. Then he put out his hand and touched Paulo's arm. Immediately Paulo felt calmer and less frightened and worried.

'No, child, I am not crazy,' Muntole said sadly. 'It is the world that is crazy – and most of all because of the evil stuff contained in this box you brought with you.' He touched the cash box lightly with his foot. 'Men fight and kill each other for money, every day, in all parts of the world. I am content to guard this sacred grove, because I believe in the holiness of life, and in living in peace with my fellow creatures, the birds, the animals and the insects. None of us has any use for wealth as the world knows it.

'Oh, yes. My brother sometimes laughs at me for staying alone here. Yet I believe that deep in his heart he envies me for being chosen as the Guardian of the Sacred Grove.'

He held Sara gently in his hand. Then he opened his fingers and the bird sat there cooing softly. Muntole rubbed her beak and smiled fondly at her.

'I promise you,' he said, 'that Sara is quite capable of delivering a message to my brother. Let me bring a pen and something to write on. The message must be short, of course, and the writing must be as tiny as possible.'

Once more, Muntole disappeared between the trees, and Paulo, worn out with crying, lay on the ground too tired to move.

When Muntole returned, carrying a narrow roll of thin paper and, surprisingly, a biro pen, Paulo was too upset to write anything and could not think what to say. Muntole sat down and, on a strip of paper no wider than the name tape sewn into the neckband of Paulo's shirt, carefully wrote the message in the tiniest of writing.

'Will this do?' he asked Paulo, and read aloud what he had written. Paulo was amazed at how much of his story Muntole had managed to cram on to such a small piece of paper. He was even more amazed to see Muntole using a thin strip of grass to attach the written message to Sara's delicate leg. Somehow Paulo had expected the bird to carry any message in her beak. He watched, open-mouthed, as Muntole whispered something to the pigeon, and she flew away obediently. She flew higher and higher in wide circles until she was above the tops of the trees. Then she flew off in a straight line as if she knew exactly where she was going.

Paulo still did not believe she would find one man in a city the size of Kampala.

'Are you sure she will find your brother?' he could not help asking.

Muntole had no doubt that Sara would deliver

Muntole used a thin strip of grass to attach the message.

the message. However, there were dangers for her to face. Birds of prey, such as kites and hawks, often attacked pigeons and wounded or killed them. But he quickly added that Sara was clever at keeping out of the way of both. Now there was nothing to do except wait. Every passing minute filled Paulo with fresh fears. He wondered whether he was being silly to trust Muntole. Was he even sillier to trust Sara's ability as a messenger? Then another thought struck him. What if all the time spent in trusting this man and his bird cost Matthew his life? How could he ever forgive himself? If he told other people they would laugh at him.

If Muntole sensed what Paulo was thinking, he gave no sign. Instead, he pointed out that the clay dressing on Paulo's ankle was dry, and suggested that Paulo might like to try walking.

'You won't be able to put your full weight on it,' he said. 'You must use your toes to take your weight. Try it.'

Paulo took a few steps, and realised that what Muntole said was true. He could walk with even greater ease after he was given the trimmed branch of a tree as a stick. He was very eager to accompany Muntole on a stroll, but then he remembered his responsibilities.

'Oh, no, I can't. How can I?' he said. 'I must stay with the cash box.'

Muntole looked down at the metal box lying between them.

'It's quite safe here,' he said quietly. 'We won't go far away. Besides, who would steal it from here? It holds nothing of interest to any of the creatures living in the Sacred Grove.'

Paulo frowned. 'Suppose somebody who doesn't belong in the Sacred Grove finds it?' he asked.

'Nobody would ever dream of entering this place with the idea of stealing anything,' Muntole declared. 'The local people respect it, for it was once the resting place of the old gods.'

Paulo did not really understand everything Muntole said. But if the local people respected this place, then no harm would come to the metal box. He was glad to set off on the walk. It helped him to forget all the trouble he was in.

They went along quite slowly because there were so many amusing and interesting things to see. Muntole pointed them out and explained them as they walked along.

For example, they came across a beautiful flower which, to Paulo's astonishment, turned out to be a flock of insects, all of the same kind but each with slightly different colouring. As soon as Muntole shook the stem, they flew into the air. Paulo was even more surprised to see the insects settle again in exactly the same order, some of them crawling over each other to get in the right place to give the 'flower' its proper colour again. Paulo had never seen anything like it.

Another amazing creature was a small, pale blue

caterpillar with a tiny red head, and a single bristle for a tail which stood upright. The caterpillar showed no alarm when Muntole touched it, but as soon as Paulo put out a finger towards it, the caterpillar drew a large green hood of skin over its head, a hood marked with two large eyes and a wide mouth.

Muntole and Paulo talked about the wonders to be seen in the wilderness, if only people would take the time to look carefully. They soon arrived at a clear spring gushing out of a great mass of black rocks. Muntole used the water to wash the clay off his face and body. Without the clay, he was a different person. Paulo now saw that Muntole's body was firm, his skin glowing with health, and his face was that of a man no older than Paulo's father. They continued their slow walk, and Paulo continued to enjoy it, although he was disappointed that they did not visit any of the holy places which Muntole occasionally mentioned. Paulo's family had been Christians for several generations, but he was curious about the gods of his forefathers, because so many of the most interesting stories told by his uncles and grandparents were about them.

At last, Muntole said that he and Paulo had walked far enough. It was important, he said, not to tire his leg too much. They sat down under a huge mango tree, and Muntole plucked some of the fruit from a low branch. Paulo pulled the skin away and took a big bite of the delicious, juicy fruit.

However, he did not take any real pleasure in the juicy mango. Neither of them had talked about Sara or her mission and Paulo had not mentioned Matthew's name again. Besides worrying about Matthew, he now imagined the brave pigeon caught in the talons of a hungry hawk. He felt guilty about leaving the responsibility for Matthew's rescue to Muntole and Sara, and wished that he had kept to his original plan of finding the nearest police post.

Muntole seemed to read Paulo's mind.

'Everything will be all right,' he said firmly. 'Fate led you to the Sacred Grove. Trust me, and trust Sara.'

He helped Paulo to his feet, and they walked slowly back to where the cash box lay untouched.

Paulo hobbled towards it, crying, 'Thank goodness it's still here. I know you said it was safe, Muntole, but I had a strange feeling that– '

Triumphant shouts drowned what he was saying. Suddenly a great many men, some of them waving pangas and others long spears, appeared from the bushes. Rongo, a cruel smile on his face, was in the middle of them.

Paulo did not see Rongo or the smile. His horrified eyes were fixed on the limp form of Matthew. He was being dragged along by the man called Joe and another member of the gang. His face was covered with blood and his clothes were torn and filthy. His eyes were closed and he did not seem to be breathing. What had happened to him? What had Rongo done to him? Was he dead? If anything had happened to Matthew, Paulo would never forgive himself.

CHAPTER NINE

Matthew had not seen the four men who attacked him until it was too late. He had been trying to find a stick for Paulo and had been staring up into the branches of the trees. He saw the men at the last moment, but by then they had tackled him and thrown him to the ground. They kicked and punched him until he was almost unconscious. Then they picked him up and, putting his arms over their shoulders, two of the men dragged him back to the road. In the darkness none of the thieves had seen Paulo sitting silently beside the cash box.

Matthew was thrown into the back of an open truck and was driven along the dirt road towards Joe's house with two of the men sitting above him. Instead of turning off at Joe's driveway, the truck drove past the entrance and on to the main road. Here it turned left on to the road along which the thieves had driven Matthew's lorry the previous night. It turned off and stopped beside the sacks of vegetables which had been thrown from Matthew's lorry.

'Well, did you get them?' Rongo shouted at the men on the back of the truck.

'We got the driver of the lorry,' one of the men answered. 'I don't know what happened to the other one.'

'Did you look for him?' Rongo shouted angrily.

'We tried, Rongo,' the man answered. 'But it was as black as the inside of a cave. We only spotted this one because he was moving around in the open.'

'All right, all right, we'll get him later,' Rongo said. 'Now, where's Joe?'

'He's coming, Rongo. He was at the house,' another man replied.

At that moment a Land Rover pulled up and Joe climbed down. He looked nervously at Rongo.

'Where's the cash box?' Rongo said in a fierce voice.

'It's hidden, like we agreed,' Joe said.

'Get it,' Rongo shouted. 'Get it now.'

'But I thought we were going to open it later,' Joe said. 'I thought it was to stay hidden.'

'Don't think, just get it,' Rongo said in the same voice. 'I want to see it.'

Joe shrugged his shoulders and walked off along the path he had taken earlier. Rongo ordered two of the men to guard Matthew and then he and the others walked quickly along the path after Joe.

When they came to the tree, Joe pushed the wild orchids to one side and crawled into the hollow trunk. Rongo and the other men looked at each other.

'It's gone! It's not here!' Joe's astonished voice came from the tree. 'Someone's taken it.' Then his voice became angry. 'Which one of you took it?

Which one of you thieves took the money?' He came rushing out from under the flowers waving his arms angrily.

'No one knew where it was, Joe,' Rongo said in a low voice, 'only you. What have you done with it, Joe?'

'Why would I take it, Rongo?' Joe asked. 'We were all going to get shares.'

'Maybe you wanted it all, Joe,' Rongo said.

He nodded at the other men and they grabbed Joe's arms and held him tightly.

'Now let's find out what happened here,' Rongo said. 'First the driver escapes, then he comes to your door. He has someone with him. Then we find him up near that old forest. But he's all alone. Is this just a story, Joe? Are you both in it together?'

'No! No! Ask my watchman, he saw them,' Joe shouted, desperately trying to pull his arms free. 'I hid the money like we agreed and then I went home. Two hours later the driver turned up at the house. He had someone with him. It looked like a boy. It was raining and you saw how dark it was yourself.'

Rongo stared at him for a long time. Then he signalled to the men holding Joe to set him free.

'I think you're telling the truth, Joe,' he said. 'I think the driver and his friend have the cash box. Come on, let's have a talk with that driver.'

Rongo turned and almost ran back to the clearing. Matthew was lying on the ground near the truck. His guards were sitting on the bonnet of the truck smoking cigarettes. Rongo shouted for them to pick Matthew up and hold him.

'Now, mister driver, you and I are going to have a little talk,' Rongo said with a smile. 'I'm going to ask you some questions and you're going to give me the answers.'

Matthew looked at Rongo, but said nothing. He was still trying to get over the beating he had been given earlier. He shook his head and tried to stand up by himself, but his legs were too weak.

'Where's the cash box and where's your young friend?' Rongo asked. 'You can answer either question. I think if we can find one of them, we'll find the other.'

Matthew said nothing. Rongo nodded and the men holding him twisted Matthew's arms up behind his back. Matthew gave a shout of pain.

'Now answer the questions or they'll really hurt you,' shouted Rongo.

'I ... don't ... know what ... you're talking a ... bout,' Matthew stammered. 'There is ... no one else.'

Rongo smiled and the men twisted Matthew's arms even harder. He screamed with the pain. Rongo watched with a cruel smile on his face. The men twisted Matthew's arms and hit him on the face and body with their fists. Still Matthew said nothing.

Then Joe saw the look on Rongo's face change. He was staring at the ground, thinking hard. When he looked up he had a pleased smile on his face. He waved his arms at the men beating Matthew.

'No, wait,' Rongo said. 'We don't need to do this. Do you remember exactly where you found him?' He spoke to the men holding Matthew.

'Yes, of course,' one of them answered. 'We found him up by the old forest near the top of Ogott's hill.'

'We'll go there in the morning,' Rongo said. 'That cash box is too heavy for a boy to carry. He'll have to pull it. All we have to do is look for the marks the box makes in the mud.' He smiled at Joe and the other men. 'You really are lucky to have someone as smart as I am. No blood, no mess. We'll find the box and the boy and then we'll kill them. The money is all ours.'

He turned back to Matthew and looked at him with a terrible smile.

'You don't have to talk,' he laughed. 'I'm just too clever for you. We'll find your friend and we'll find the box. Don't you worry.' He walked over to the Land Rover. 'All right, we'll go back to your house, Joe. As soon as it's daylight, we'll drive up to that forest of yours.'

The vehicles turned and drove back along the track to the road. They were soon driving into Joe's driveway. They parked along either side of the path. The rain had stopped and the clouds had blown away. The moon shone quite brightly.

'Some hot food and a drink is what we need,'

Rongo said, smiling happily. 'Come on, Joe. Be happy. The money will soon be ours.'

Rongo put his arm around Joe's shoulders and they went into the house together.

◇

As soon as the sun rose, Rongo and the other thieves climbed into the Land Rovers and the truck and drove towards Ogott's hill. Some of them had thrown Matthew into the back of the truck again and sat with their feet on him.

They parked their vehicles at the top of the hill and stood along the edge of the road. Rongo climbed up the bank and looked down at the forest.

'Spread out in a line,' he said, 'and keep your eyes open. We're looking for the marks a heavy box would make if someone was pulling it along the ground. Joe, you and Petro bring the driver. I want him to see this.'

They walked down the hill in a long line, peering at the ground. The line went down past the forest and came to the thick hedge of elephant grass. There were no marks to be seen.

'The rain was very heavy, Rongo,' one of the men said. 'Maybe it washed the marks away.'

'No. This mud is quite hard,' Rongo replied. 'We'll find them, don't you worry. Just keep looking.'

They moved nearer the forest and spread out

again. When they reached the top of the hill, some of the men were panting heavily. Joe had been sitting down, watching Rongo while he guarded Matthew.

'There are no marks, Rongo,' Joe said. 'We're wasting our time climbing up and down this hill.'

'Just keep looking. We'll find them,' Rongo shouted in a rage. 'Come on, move over a bit, right next to the forest.'

The line moved slowly down the hill again. The men were tired, but they wanted to find the box. They wanted the money in the box. Suddenly there was a shout and one of the men pointed at the ground in front of him. Then another man shouted and pointed. Soon five of them were looking down at the two deep tracks in the ground.

'Well, didn't I tell you?' Rongo asked. 'Didn't I tell you? They put the box down here and when you caught the driver, the boy pulled the box into the forest. Come on, let's find him.'

Rongo waved for Joe to bring Matthew down. He waited until the three men had joined them. Then he pointed at the tracks.

'So there are no marks, Joe,' Rongo laughed. 'The rain washed them away, Joe. Now tell me Rongo's wrong.'

Joe stared at the tracks and then looked at Rongo. He shrugged his shoulders.

'You were lucky this time,' he said. 'Now stop showing off and find that box.'

Then he pointed at the tracks.

Rongo laughed at him again and turned to follow the tracks.

'I'll bet you half my share,' he said, 'that we find the box and the boy in the next half hour.'

He pointed into the forest and then waved for the men to follow him.

CHAPTER TEN

'You see. I was right, as usual,' Rongo boasted to Joe. 'When you came and told me about a man calling at your house, and then when we discovered that the cash box was gone from where you had hidden it, it didn't take me long to work out what had happened. It was obvious. The boy would try to pull the box to a place of safety. All we had to do was find the tracks made by the box being dragged through the mud.

'If it hadn't been for me, none of you would have been able to follow the clues. I knew that if we could find the tracks, they would lead us straight to the cash box.'

Paulo, when he managed to take his eyes off Matthew, noticed that Joe was sweating, and that his mouth was twitching nervously.

'Don't waste time telling us how clever you are,' Joe said quickly to Rongo. 'Let's get out of this place – you must know that it's haunted?' He threw a frightened glance at Muntole. 'Besides, terrible things will happen to all of us if that one comes to any harm.'

Rongo laughed scornfully. 'You and your superstitions! Anybody can see that the man is an ignorant savage. We'll have to make sure he never talks – him and the lorry driver and this schoolboy. They must never get the chance to tell the police what they know about us.'

'No, I'll have no part in killing anybody,' Joe replied firmly.

Rongo glared at him, and said, 'What are you talking about? We're all in this together, and you'll do what you're told. We can't leave these three to talk to the police. If you're worried about your share of the money, we'll open the box now, and you can take your share.'

'I won't touch stolen money in this place,' Joe told him. 'Listen to reason, Rongo. There's been one problem after another with this job. I'm beginning to think it was unlucky right from the start. Let's take the box and open it in the workshop where we have the tools, and let's leave these three people alone.'

'What?' laughed Rongo. 'Leave them here so that they can run to the police as soon as our backs are turned? Joe, you must be mad! No. The sooner we finish this job the better. It's already gone on too long. I'm going to shoot the lock off the box. Then we can share out the money, and I'll take care of these three.'

Joe released his hold on Matthew, so that Matthew half fell to the ground. Then he rushed over to Rongo, shouting, 'Don't you understand? This place is haunted by the old gods. Some of their holy places are still here!'

The rest of the gang moved their feet uneasily, and began talking quietly among themselves. When one standing near Paulo suddenly started trembling and making a choking noise in his throat, the others clung together in a terrified group. They turned to run as the man fell to the ground, jerking his limbs and frothing at the mouth.

A shot fired in the air from the gun Rongo had pulled out of his pocket halted the men at once. They stopped as though turned to stone. For a moment there was a complete silence, broken by somebody whispering, 'See, our brother is bewitched!'

'Not bewitched. He's having a fit,' Muntole explained quietly. The men watched with terror in their eyes and nobody prevented him from attending the poor man who jerked and frothed on the ground.

As if by magic, Muntole rapidly made a small bundle of twigs, and placed it between the man's teeth. This, he quietly explained to everyone watching, was to save the man's tongue from being chewed to pieces, or rolling back into his throat and choking him.

The man soon recovered, but he continued to lie, exhausted, where he had fallen.

Rongo ignored him. Waving the gun, he said, 'The show is over, and there was no witchcraft. Now I'm going to shoot the lock off this box, and give everybody what I agreed to pay them.'

He knelt to examine the lock on the cash box.

Just at that moment Paulo caught sight of the man Petro, and he shivered at the strange look on

Petro's face. As he stared at him, Paulo realised that Petro was pulling a small gun out of the pocket of his jacket. Before Paulo could do anything, Petro aimed the gun straight at Rongo's back.

Muntole's eyes followed Paulo's frightened gaze and saw what was about to happen. He quickly put out his hand and touched Petro's arm.

Petro was startled by Muntole's touch. He swung round to face him, and pushed him away. Muntole quickly raised one hand.

'This is the Sacred Grove,' he said, still looking at Petro. 'Evil will come to the person who sheds blood here.' Rongo heard him, and turned to ask what was going on. His eyes widened in terror as he saw the gun pointed at him.

'Come away from that box,' Petro ordered him. 'We've had enough of you. I suppose we are already cursed for trying to hurt the Guardian of the Sacred Grove, but there is no reason to make matters worse by sharing out stolen money in this place.'

Rongo, like a trapped animal, looked here and there to see if he had any supporters among the gang of frightened men. His own gun hung loosely in his hand, and when Petro told him to drop it, he let it fall. He looked at Petro with a pleading look on his face.

'What's going on, Petro?' he said sadly. 'I thought you were my friend. I trusted you, and I always believed you trusted me.'

His eyes widened in terror as he saw the gun pointed at him.

'I did trust you,' Petro replied, 'but I won't ever trust you again. You've led us into too much trouble in the last few months. My brother is in prison because of you. Lately, you've shown you're not fit to lead us. You've become too boastful. You think you're smarter than anyone else. We'll do as Joe suggested, and take the box to the workshop, and...'

Because Rongo had dropped his gun, Petro no longer pointed his own weapon at him. Everybody was taken completely by surprise when Rongo, in one swift movement, picked up his gun and pointed it at Petro.

Paulo was never clear about what happened next. He saw Muntole throw himself in front of Petro. Then he heard a shot, and was aware of Rongo screaming and rolling on the ground. Blood was pouring from his hand, and the pistol had fallen to the ground. He held his hand against his body to try to stop the flow of blood.

The rest was a confused mixture of shouts and whistles. Then just as suddenly, uniformed police seemed to spring like magic out of the surrounding bushes.

Within minutes, the gang was being led away. This included Rongo, Petro and Joe, and the other two 'bosses' whose names Paulo never learned. Two policemen knelt beside Matthew who sat up and grinned when Paulo hurried to him.

'Is he badly hurt?' Paulo asked the policemen.

'Of course I'm not!' Matthew answered. 'I'm worn out through lack of sleep, that's all.'

'I think we'd better have you checked over by a doctor,' one of the policemen remarked. 'That's a nasty bruise on the side of your head.'

Matthew protested that he would soon be all right, but in the end agreed to be taken for treatment at the nearest hospital. Before he climbed into a police car, he reminded Paulo to tell the police everything he knew about the old man, Kaddana.

'He's as guilty as Rongo and the others,' Matthew said. 'He was going to steal the money his friends had been saving.'

Muntole had slipped out of sight as soon as the police had started to run into the clearing. He reappeared in the company of a police officer just as Matthew was being helped from the grove.

Muntole laughed as he introduced Paulo to his brother.

'I told you everything would be all right,' he said, 'and that my brother would be here by noon.'

Paulo glanced at the sky, and saw the sun shining directly overhead. The police officer smiled down at him.

'I'm Muntole's brother, Chief Inspector Kakoza, and we're all very grateful to you, young man, for your part in helping us catch that gang. They have given us a lot of trouble lately.'

He shook hands with Paulo and explained that the gang had been stealing money and cattle for months. They had been suspicious of Joe and some of the other men, but they had never managed to get enough evidence to arrest them.

Paulo looked around the clearing as if he was searching for something.

'What about Sara the pigeon?' he asked the police officer. 'Is she all right? Did she arrive safely?'

Chief Inspector Kakoza laughed and looked at his brother.

'Sara is fine,' he said. 'At the moment she is sleeping in one of her favourite places – the glove compartment of my Land Rover. No, don't ask me how she does it. I'm always surprised when she lands on the windowsill or flies into my Land Rover.'

'It's wonderful that a little bird can deliver messages!' Paulo exclaimed.

'Not all that wonderful for a pigeon,' Muntole said. 'In many parts of the world, pigeons have been famous as messengers for centuries.'

Paulo would have liked to hear more about how pigeons deliver messages, and was just about to ask Muntole to explain how they knew where to go. Before he could speak the chief inspector took his arm gently.

'I want you to come to the Kampala Central Police Station and write down everything you remember about what has happened since last night,' he said. 'We'll get in touch with your parents to tell them that you're safe. Then we'll get you some food and I'll drive you home. I want to tell your mother and father how brave you were.'

When the chief inspector began to talk about food, Paulo realised just how hungry he was. Muntole's bread and honey had been good, but he needed a real meal to make him feel right again.

'I'll go to the Land Rover and bring Sara back to the grove,' said the chief inspector, 'and while I'm there, I'll get two of the constables to come for this cash box.'

As soon as he had gone, Paulo grasped Muntole's hand and held it hard.

'Oh, Muntole, how can I thank you for all you have done for me?' he said. 'I don't know what would have happened if you hadn't found me.'

'Stop worrying,' Muntole told him. 'It's all over and you're quite safe. You were a very brave young man, you know. Your parents should be proud of you. I know they're worried and frightened, but when they hear what you did, they'll be proud. And don't forget, whenever you wish to escape from the madness of the world or whenever you're tired or unhappy, come back here to us in the Sacred Grove. My friends and I will always be happy to welcome you.'

Paulo could feel tears stinging the backs of his eyes. He could only nod his head and shake

Muntole's hand again. Then once again Muntole slipped among the trees and disappeared from view.

The chief inspector was soon back with two constables who picked up the cash box and carried it away. Sara was sitting happily on the chief inspector's shoulder. She looked at Paulo for a moment and then flew to perch on his shoulder and coo a pigeon secret in his ear. She looked around again and flew off in the direction Muntole had taken.

'Time for us to go, young man,' the chief inspector said. 'It will take us an hour to write your statement and then we'll have a really good meal. I can't wait to see your parents' faces when we tell them about your adventure.'

Although Paulo was glad to be going home, he was suddenly sad at having to leave the Sacred Grove. It was a strange, secret place, and it was very mysterious. But it was so peaceful and quiet.

As the Land Rover turned out on to the main road, Paulo thought for the first time about his friends Richard and Basil. They wouldn't believe what had happened to him. No, they would never believe his strange adventure. But he would tell them all about it. It had certainly been more exciting than climbing a silly old ladder!

Questions

1 What reason does Paulo give for not wanting to climb the ladder?

2 What happens when he does climb the ladder?

3 How does Paulo meet Matthew?

4 Why is the lorry carrying a box full of money?

5 How did Paulo know where Joe had hidden the box?

6 Why are Matthew and Paulo surprised when they go to the house for help?

7 Who is Muntole? What is his job?

8 Why is Joe frightened to share out the money in the Sacred Grove?

9 How are the police able to arrive in time to catch the thieves?

Activities

1 Draw a picture of Paulo **either** as he is about to fall off the ladder, **or** after he has fallen into the lorry.

2 Could you write a short, funny story about a boy or a girl who falls off a ladder? Explain why they are on the ladder, why they fall off and what happens to them after they fall.

Glossary

clenching (page 3) holding your teeth tightly together

drenching (page 5) getting very, very wet

frothing (page 78) lots of little bubbles coming out of his mouth

gigantic (page 22) very big, huge

godown (page 15) another name for a warehouse, or a large store

grimy (page 23) dirty, covered in grease and dirt

guardian (page 51) someone who looks after a place or a person

kanzu (page 23) a man's long shirt

kikoyi (page 17) a skirt worn by men. It is a long piece of cloth wrapped around the waist which reaches down to the ankles

posho (page 17) porridge

sacred grove (page 51) a small wood or forest in which people believe the gods live or lived

scornfully (page 76) speaking to someone without any respect for them, contemptuously

shamba (page 2) a large vegetable garden

starvation (page 34) dying from lack of food

statement (page 85) this is what you tell the police if you have seen or are involved in a robbery or an accident

stunned (page 5) knocked almost unconscious

tailboard (page 8) the piece of wood at the back of a lorry which can be raised to prevent things sliding off

timidly (page 1) in a shy way, when you are easily frightened

triumphant (page 65) knowing that you have won, victorious

Other books in the Junior African Writers Series

Level 4

Street Gang Kid

Shirley Bojé

Vikani finds himself destitute after his house is attacked and burnt down. He is forced to join a street gang and is then arrested by the police.

0 435 89298 3   96pp

Follow the Crow

Hugh Lewin

How did the police discover that a fugitive was hiding in the village? Can he escape with the help of the local boys?

0 435 89299 1   80pp

The Secret Valley

Mike Sadler

Bupe and his father, an education officer in Northern Zambia, try to discover why children in a remote country area are disappearing. Then Bupe disappears too.

0 435 89300 9   96pp

The Innocent Prisoner

Kwasi Koranteng

Brakwa is about to fly to the United States when an airport security man arrests him. Cocaine is found in his suitcase. Who put it there? How can Brakwa prove he is innocent?

0 435 89293 2   96pp

The Junior African Writers Series is designed to provide interesting and varied African stories either for pleasure or for study. There are five graded levels in the series at present.

Level 4 prepares readers moving on to unsimplified books in English. The content and language remain carefully controlled to increase fluency in reading

Content The stories are adult, dealing with contemporary themes and issues, but the information is presented in a clear and straightforward way. Chapters divide the stories into focused episodes and the illustrations help to set the scenes.

Language Reading is a learning experience and, although the choice of words is carefully controlled (basic vocabulary level of about 1750 words), new words, important to the story, are also introduced. These are contextualised, recycled through the story and explained in the glossary. The sentences are balanced and sentence length is limited to a maximum of four clauses.

Glossary Difficult words which learners may not know and which are not made clear in the text or illustrations have been listed alphabetically at the back of the book. The definitions refer to the way the word is used in the story and the page reference is for the word's first use.

Questions and **Activities** The questions give useful comprehension practice and ensure that the reader has followed and understood the story. The activities develop themes and ideas introduced and can be done as pairwork or groupwork in class, or as homework.